CAPTAIN AWESOME

VS. THE EVIL ICE CREAM JINGLE

By STAN KIRBY

Illustrated by DOC MORAN

LITTLE SIMON
New York   London   Toronto   Sydney   New Delhi

LITTLE SIMON

An imprint of Simon & Schuster Children's Publishing Division • 1230 Avenue of the Americas, New York, New York 10020 • First Little Simon paperback edition June 2022 • Copyright © 2022 by Simon & Schuster, Inc. • Also available in a Little Simon hardcover edition. • All rights reserved, including the right of reproduction in whole or in part in any form. • LITTLE SIMON is a registered trademark of Simon & Schuster, Inc., and associated colophon is a trademark of Simon & Schuster, Inc. • For information about special discounts for bulk purchases, please contact Simon & Schuster Special Sales at 1-866-506-1949 or business@simonandschuster.com. • The Simon & Schuster Speakers Bureau can bring authors to your live event. • For more information or to book an event, contact the Simon & Schuster Speakers Bureau at 1-866-248-3049 or visit our website at www.simonspeakers.com. • Designed by Chani Yammer. • The text of this book was set in Little Simon Gazette.

Manufactured in the United States of America 0522 MTN

10 9 8 7 6 5 4 3 2 1

Library of Congress Cataloging-in-Publication Data

Names: Kirby, Stan, author. | Moran, Doc, illustrator. | Title: Captain Awesome vs. the evil ice cream jingle / by Stan Kirby ; illustrated by Doc Moran. | Description: First Little Simon paperback edition. | New York : Little Simon, 2022. | Series: Captain Awesome ; 24 | Audience: Ages 5–9. | Summary: When Bob shows up in his ice cream truck something is different about him, and Captain Awesome and the Sunnyview Superhero Squad are convinced that this can only mean one thing—Bob has an evil Ice Cream Clone. | Identifiers: LCCN 2021051336 (print) | LCCN 2021051337 (ebook) | ISBN 9781665916950 (paperback) | ISBN 9781665916967 (hardcover) | ISBN 9781665916974 (ebook) | Subjects: CYAC: Superheroes—Fiction. | Ice cream trucks—Fiction. | Fiction. lcgft | Classification: LCC PZ7.K633529 Cbg 2022 (print) | LCC PZ7.K633529 (ebook) | DDC [E]—dc23

LC record available at https://lccn.loc.gov/2021051336

Table of Contents

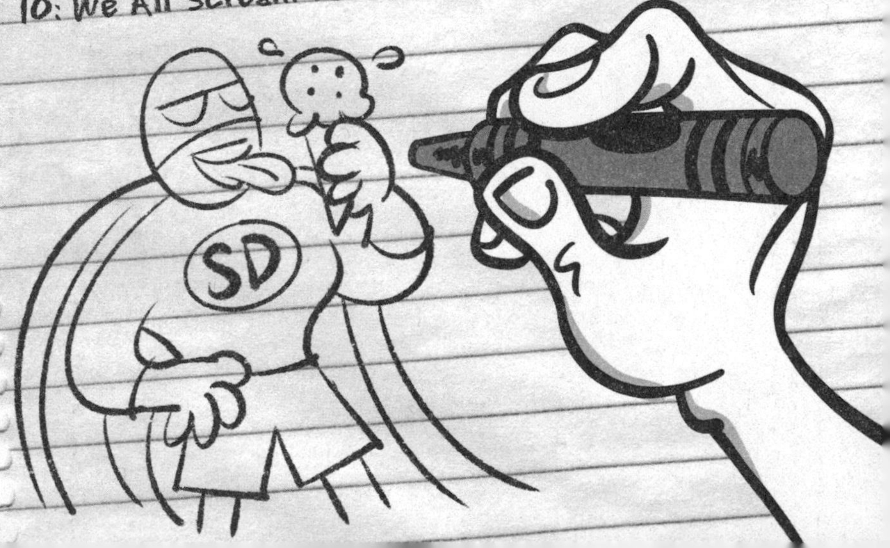

SD

CHAPTER 1

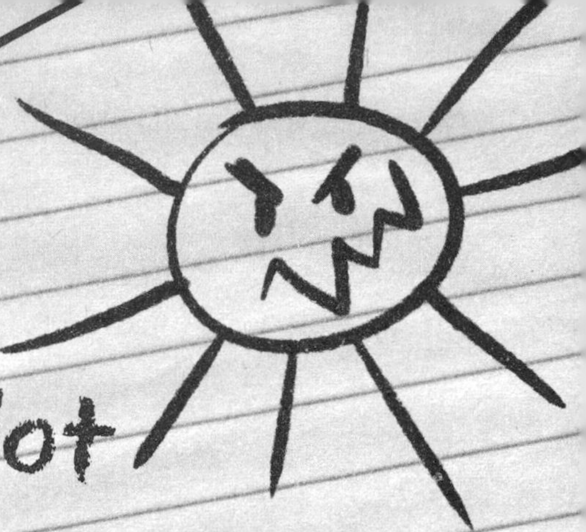

Is It Hot Enough for You?

By Eugene

"Is the egg cooked yet?"
Eugene McGillicudy asked his best
friend Charlie Thomas Jones. They
watched as a freshly cracked egg
sizzled on the hot patio in Eugene's
backyard.

"Nope, it's still runny and
goopy," Charlie answered. "Only my
dad would eat it this way." Then he
leaned down for a closer look. "Ew,
there's also a fly in it. Even my dad
wouldn't eat this."

1

"Maybe frying an egg on the patio isn't a good idea," Eugene said, taking a giant slurp of his mom's homemade lemonade.

SLURP!
SLURP!
SLURRRRRP!

"Hold on. The meteor . . . meaty. . . uh, weatherperson said today was hot enough to cook an egg," Charlie said. "We both heard it!"

Then he squirted a blast of canned cheese into his mouth. "Yeah, it's so hot right now, not even spearmint nacho cheese can cool me off."

"Oh no, hurry! It's time to shade-shift!" Eugene cried out.

Eugene and Charlie stood up, held their lawn chairs to their butts, and scooted five steps to the left to

get back into the shade. It was so hot, the boys were only wearing their bathing suits.

"Aahhhhhhh!" they sighed as they leaned back. "That's better."

Right then, Mr. McGillicudy, Eugene's dad, stepped out the back door holding a sprinkler over his head like it was a sword pulled from a magic stone. "Hey, Eugene, I found your Super Dude Water Sprinkler!"

He attached the sprinkler to a long hose and set it down on the lawn. A smiling Super Dude action figure was mounted on top.

"Get ready to run through cold Super Dude sprinkled water!" Eugene's dad said proudly.

"WOO-HOOOOOO! Super Dude sprinkled water!" the two boys cheered. Their eyes grew wide as they waited.

Wait a minute. What's that, you say? You've never heard of **Super Dude**, the greatest comic book character of all time? Well, inspired by the adventures of their favorite comic book hero, Eugene, Charlie, and their best friend, Sally Williams, adopted secret identities.

Together, they are Sunnyview's leading superheroes: **Captain Awesome**, **Nacho Cheese Man**, and **Supersonic Sal**. It's their job to keep Sunnyview safe from creepy monsters and bad guys made of hot lava.

"Do you want it on sprinkle, more sprinkle, or super sprinkle?" Eugene's dad asked.

"Super sprinkle!" they cried.

Eugene's dad nodded and turned the faucet. But instead of shooting out like a rocket, the water trickled out in small, weak bursts.

WHOMP!
WHOMP!
WHOMP!

And then the sprinkler died.

"NOOOOO! Super Dude would never let us down like this!" Eugene yelled. "I know! It's not too late. All we need are Super Dude's Icy-Cold Water Blasters that he used to cool down the Flaming Monster of Moongor in Super Dude number five!"

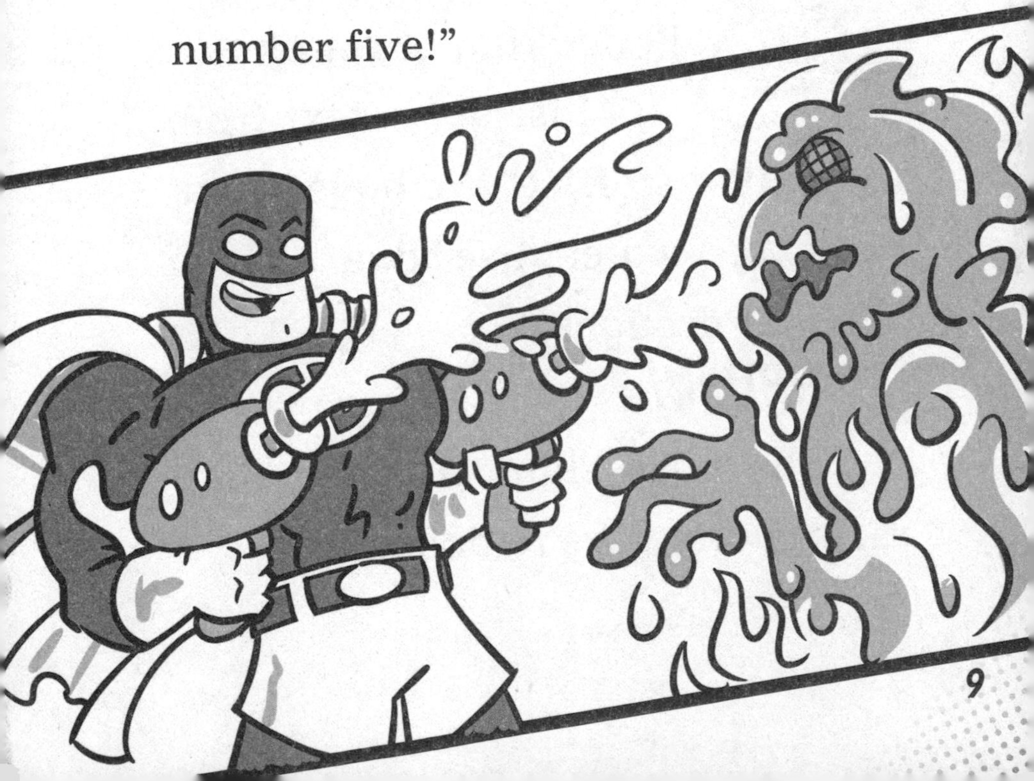

"Totally!" Charlie agreed. "That flaming monster melted like hot cheese!"

PING!

"Um, sorry, boys, there's bad news," Mr. McGillicudy said, looking at his phone. "Just got a text from the mayor's office. We have to cut back on water use due to the summer drought."

GROAN!

The boys slumped down into their chairs. "We're doomed!"

But the next second, Eugene and Charlie both perked up.

TING-TING! TA-TING! TING-TING!

"Look! It's the ice cream truck!" Charlie yelled, leaping off his chair like a rocket.

"Hey, Dad, can we have some money?" Eugene asked. "I promise I'll do all my chores without being told!"

"Deal!" Eugene's dad said, handing him a ten-dollar bill. "But if the ice cream man comes again, it's extra chores for you!"

"You got it! Thanks, Dad!" Eugene said. "Time for ice cream coolness!"

Eugene and Charlie then ran down the street at top speed.

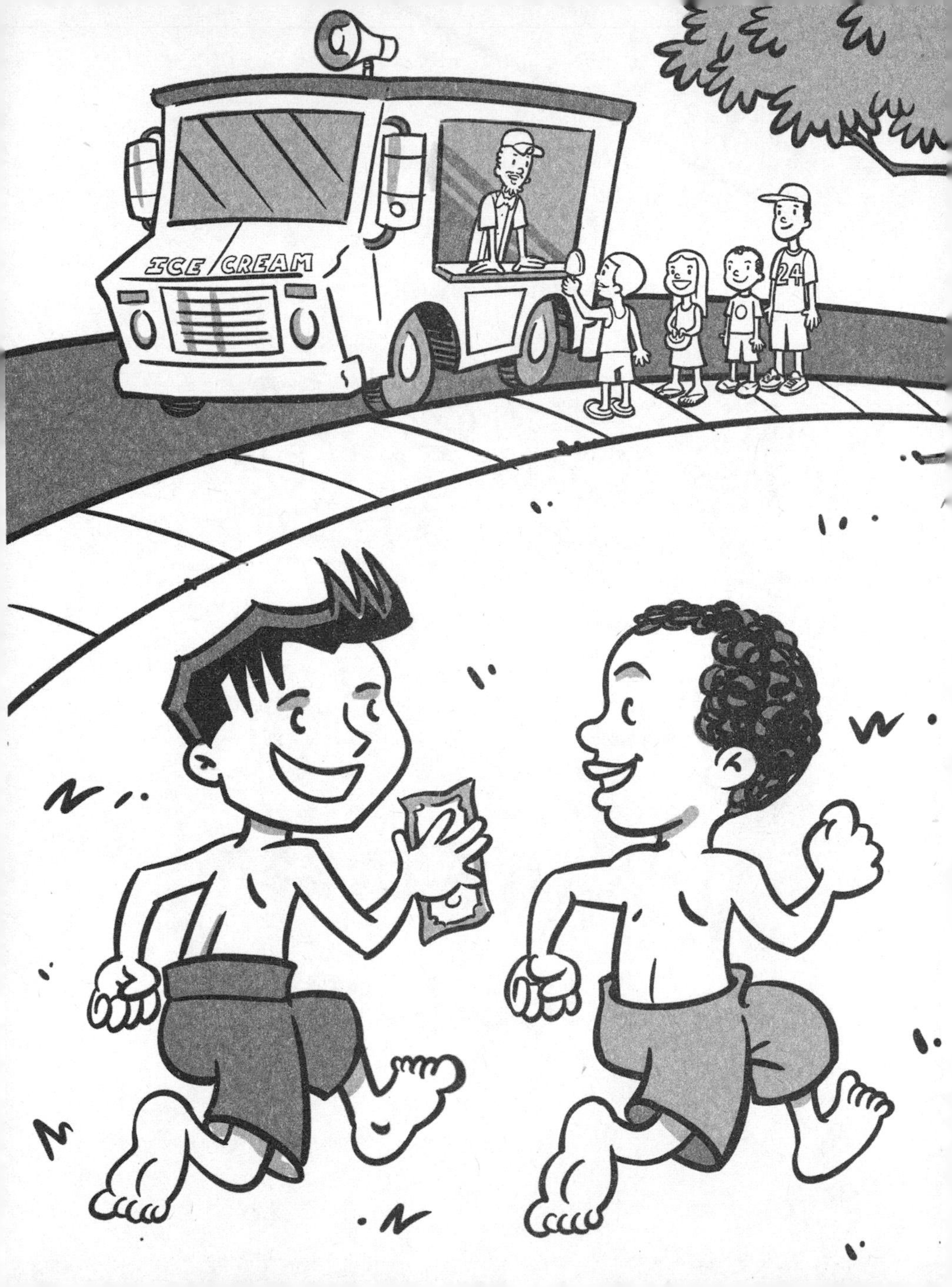
ICE CREAM
24

CHAPTER 2

We All Scream for Ice Cream!

By
Eugene

There was a long line at Bob's Ice Cream Truck. But finally the ice cream man poked his head out from the large window. He wore a white shirt with a polka-dot bow tie.

"Hey there! What'll you boys be having?" he asked Eugene and Charlie. "I've got Icy-Cold Ice Cream, Double-Pop Popsicles, Mister Freezies, Fruit Whipple-Dipples, Chocolate Banana Blasters—you name it!"

"That sounds awesome," Eugene said. "But I'll have my usual!"

"And what would your usual be, young man?" the man asked.

Hmm, that's strange. Bob always knows what I get every day! Eugene thought. *But his brain must*

be melting thanks to the heat.

"Oh, one Chocoberry Taco, please," Eugene said with a smile.

"And I'll have a Fireworks Popsicle with extra works!" Charlie added.

The ice cream man handed the boys their frozen treats. Then Eugene paid for them and thanked him. Charlie eagerly ripped off the wrapper and took the first lick.

"The chill of a thousand pops in one 'sicle!" Charlie declared. He licked again and again until he stopped. "AHHHHH! BRAIN FREEZE!"

Charlie twisted and turned like a frozen pretzel. He closed his eyes tightly. "Eugene! You must. Unfreeze. My brain!" he huffed in between breaths.

"Let me secretly use my Captain Awesome powers!" Eugene said.

Then he patted Charlie's head over and over.

Charlie's legs wobbled, and his arms drooped like spaghetti. But within seconds, it worked!

"Whew, thanks!" he cried. "I feel better! And much cooler now. But you know what would be even cooler?"

"What?"

"The pool!" Charlie exclaimed.

Eugene jumped up and gave his best friend a high five. That was the best idea they'd had all day!

Eugene took the last bite of his Chocoberry Taco before looking over at his friend.

"Hey, was there something a bit funny about Bob, the ice cream man, today?" he asked.

"Well, I *did* get brain freeze," Charlie said. "What's up with that?"

Eugene laughed as he kept thinking.

"Aha! POLKA DOTS!"

Eugene finally shouted. “His bow tie had polka dots!”

“What’s wrong with that?” Charlie asked.

“Bob always wears a *striped* bow tie. He’s not a polka-dot guy!”

“Maybe he’s trying a new style,” Charlie said. “Like that time I was going to add my favorite top hat to my Nacho Cheese Man costume.”

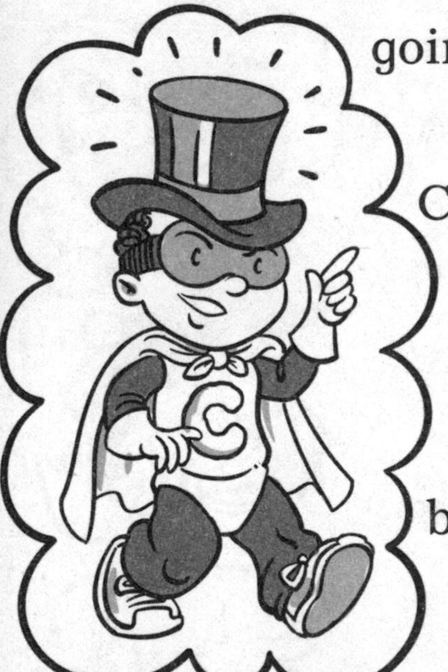

Charlie smiled. “I have to admit, it wasn’t a great idea, but I *did* like that hat.”

"Yeah, I guess you're right about the tie," Eugene agreed. "Just please don't bring that hat to the pool," he added with a smirk.

The boys laughed. Then they raced home to get their swim gear and some extra ice cream money, just in case.

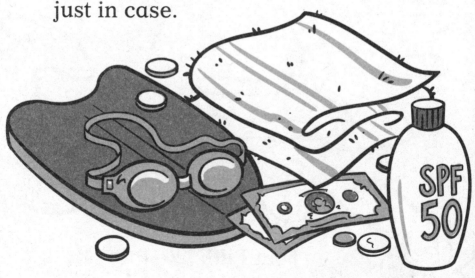

CHAPTER 3

Pool Time!

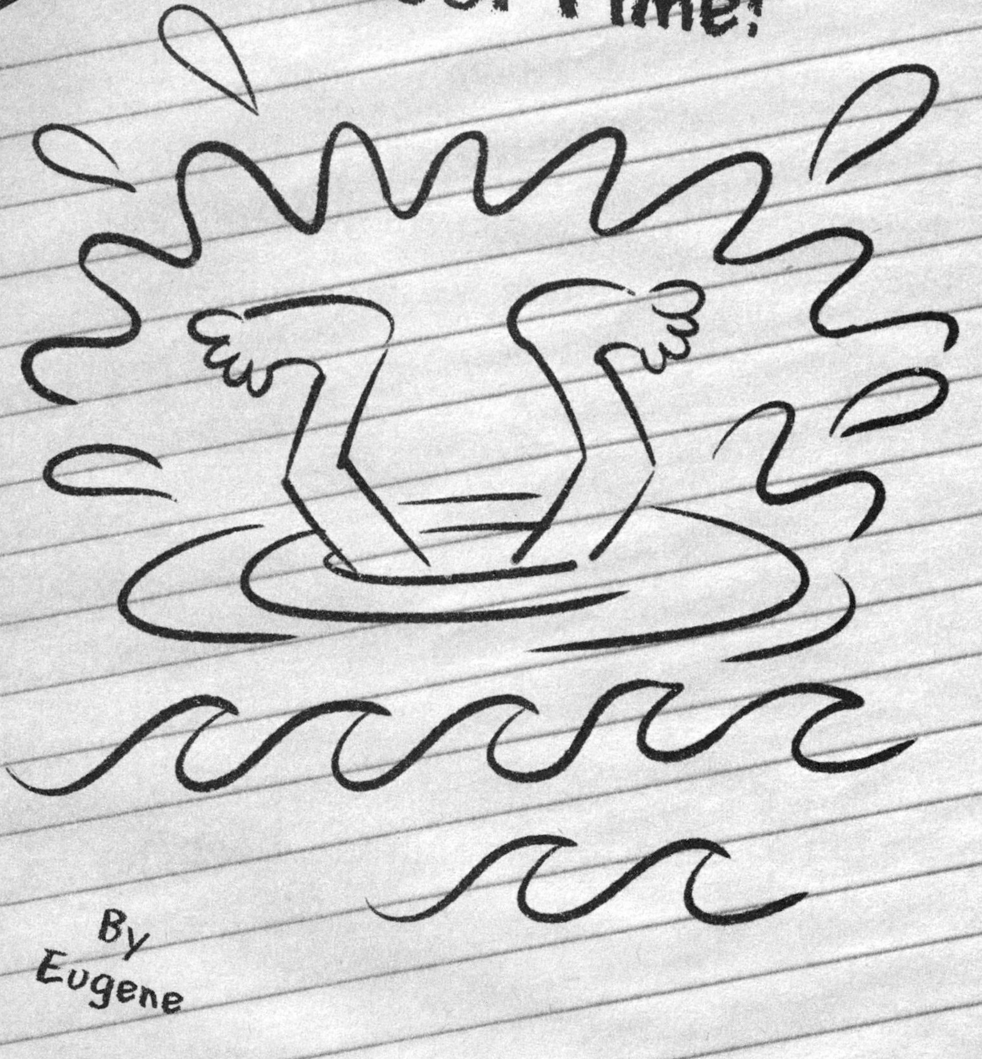

By
Eugene

Eugene put on his Super Dude swim goggles and dove into the pool. He landed on his Super Dude inner tube with a big **SPLASH!**

"This is awesome!" Eugene cheered. "Nothing beats ice cream and a day at the pool!"

Charlie swam next to him on a bright yellow float, the color of nacho cheese.

"And if we're super lucky, we'll get a second ice cream today when

Bob's Ice Cream Truck stops here," Charlie said. "But stay close in case my brain freezes again!" Charlie gulped down a cool blast of spearmint nacho cheese from his spray can.

"Okay, but when he shows up, check out Bob's bow tie and see if

I'm right about the polka dots,"
Eugene said.

"Look for polka dots. Got it!
My Nacho Cheese Man powers of
observation still work even when
I'm not in my supersuit," Charlie
replied.

GASP! SHOCK! MYSTERY!

"There's something else!" Eugene said. "Bob didn't have his glasses on! Bob always wears glasses!"

Before Charlie could respond, they were both splashed by a pink sea monster.

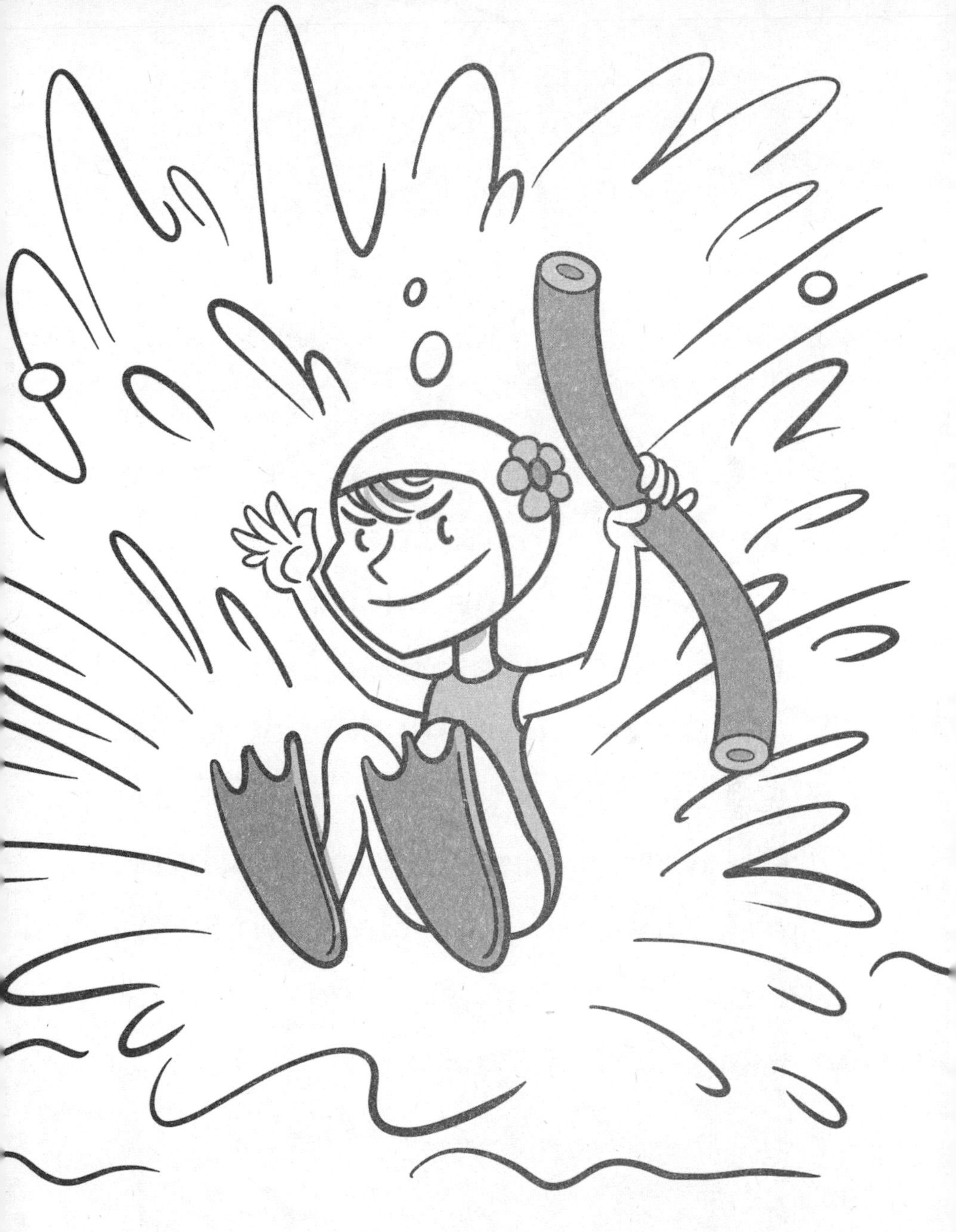

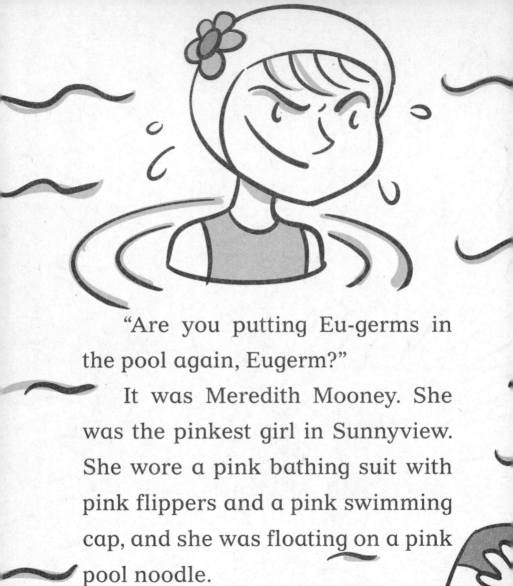

"Are you putting Eu-germs in the pool again, Eugerm?"

It was Meredith Mooney. She was the pinkest girl in Sunnyview. She wore a pink bathing suit with pink flippers and a pink swimming cap, and she was floating on a pink pool noodle.

"What do you call that float? A Super Dupe?" she said with a sneer.

"Leave us alone, because I'm going to do . . . a dive bomb!" Eugene yelled. He rolled off his Super Dude float and splashed Meredith right back.

"Hmph!" Meredith groaned. Then she waded over to the other side of the pool.

Charlie gave his friend a thumbs-up as Eugene came to the

surface. And just like they'd hoped, that's when they heard it again.

TING-TING! TA-TING! TING-TING!

The jingle of the ice cream truck! Bob was here!

They ran out to the parking lot as the ice cream truck sped by. The truck wasn't stopping!

"The ice cream truck always stops at the pool," Eugene said, confused.

Charlie pointed ahead. "Wait! He's coming back!"

And he was. But the truck

turned around and drove past them
in the other direction!

ZOOOOOOM!

"Man, Bob is acting so weird
today!" Eugene said.

"Yeah, not sure what's going on
with him. But on the upside," Charlie
said, "at least you won't have to do
any extra chores!"

CHAPTER 4

Ice Cream
Hide-and-Seek

By
Eugene

But then the downside kicked in.

"Aw, shucks! Does that mean we don't get a second ice cream?" Charlie groaned. "This is totally *not* the best part of a hot day."

"It's more like the worst part of a not-so-great day!" Eugene complained. "It's a scientific fact that Chocoberry Tacos taste the best after swimming!"

"Yeah, Sally says that all the time too!" Charlie agreed. So with that, they decided to pack up their things and bike to her house.

When they arrived, **Sally Williams** was sitting on her front porch, petting her cat, **Mr. Whiskersworth.**

“Hey, Sally!” Eugene called out. “Have you seen the ice cream truck?”

“Have I ever!” Sally said. “He’s been driving past my house for the last thirty minutes.”

She pointed down her street.

“And here he comes again,” she added. “But he never stops!”

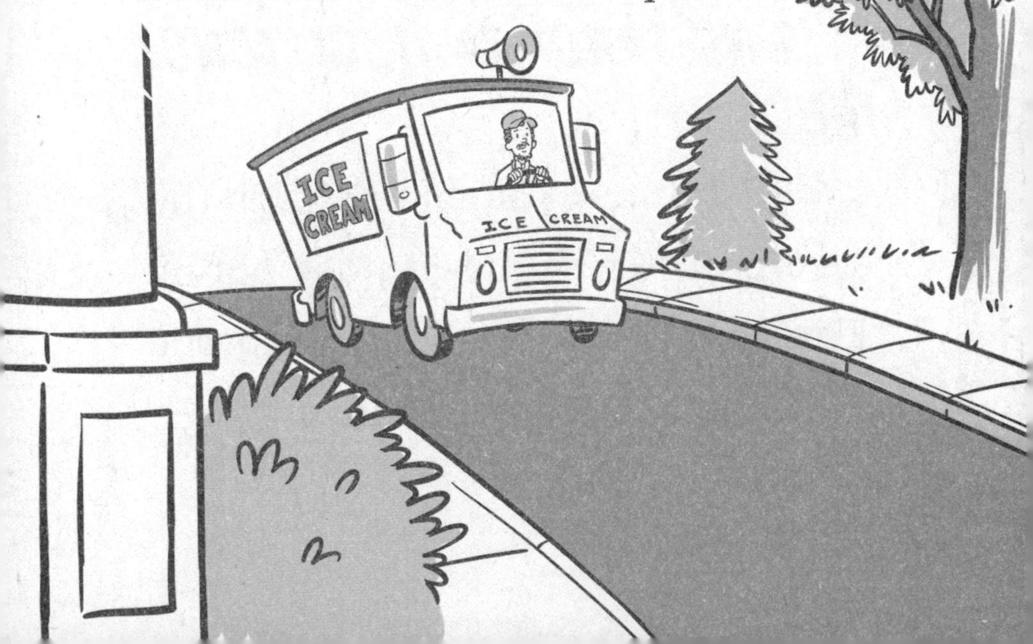
ICE CREAM
ICE CREAM

TING-TING! TA-TING! TONG-TANG!

"Bob's been acting weird all day. He didn't stop at the pool, either," Eugene said. "We should hide and see what he does!"

Eugene, Charlie, Sally, and Mr. Whiskersworth ran behind the bushes in Sally's front yard.

TING-TONG! TA-TING! TONG-TANG!

"Listen up," Eugene said as the ice cream truck drove past again. "The jingle isn't even jingling the right jingle. It sounds evil!"

"It sounds like it's playing upside down," Charlie said. "My piano teacher would give him extra homework!"

The ice cream truck stopped three houses down, then drove back.

"Hey, he's coming back!" Sally said.

They dropped behind the bushes as the ice cream truck drove past them again.

TING-TONG! TA-TING! TONG-TANG!

The truck turned right at the corner and disappeared. Eugene, Charlie, and Sally popped up from behind the bushes.

"There's something off for sure. The truck is playing an evil jingle, it's driving a weird route, and I swear, Bob's not even wearing his glasses or his striped bow tie!"

"And he made my brain freeze!"
Charlie added.

"This can only mean one thing!"
Eugene cried. "Bob's been replaced
by the most coldhearted, yet tasty,
supervillain of them all . . . **the Evil
Ice Cream Clone!**"

Sally looked up and stopped
petting Mr. Whiskersworth. "This
sounds like a job for the

Sunnyview Superhero Squad!"

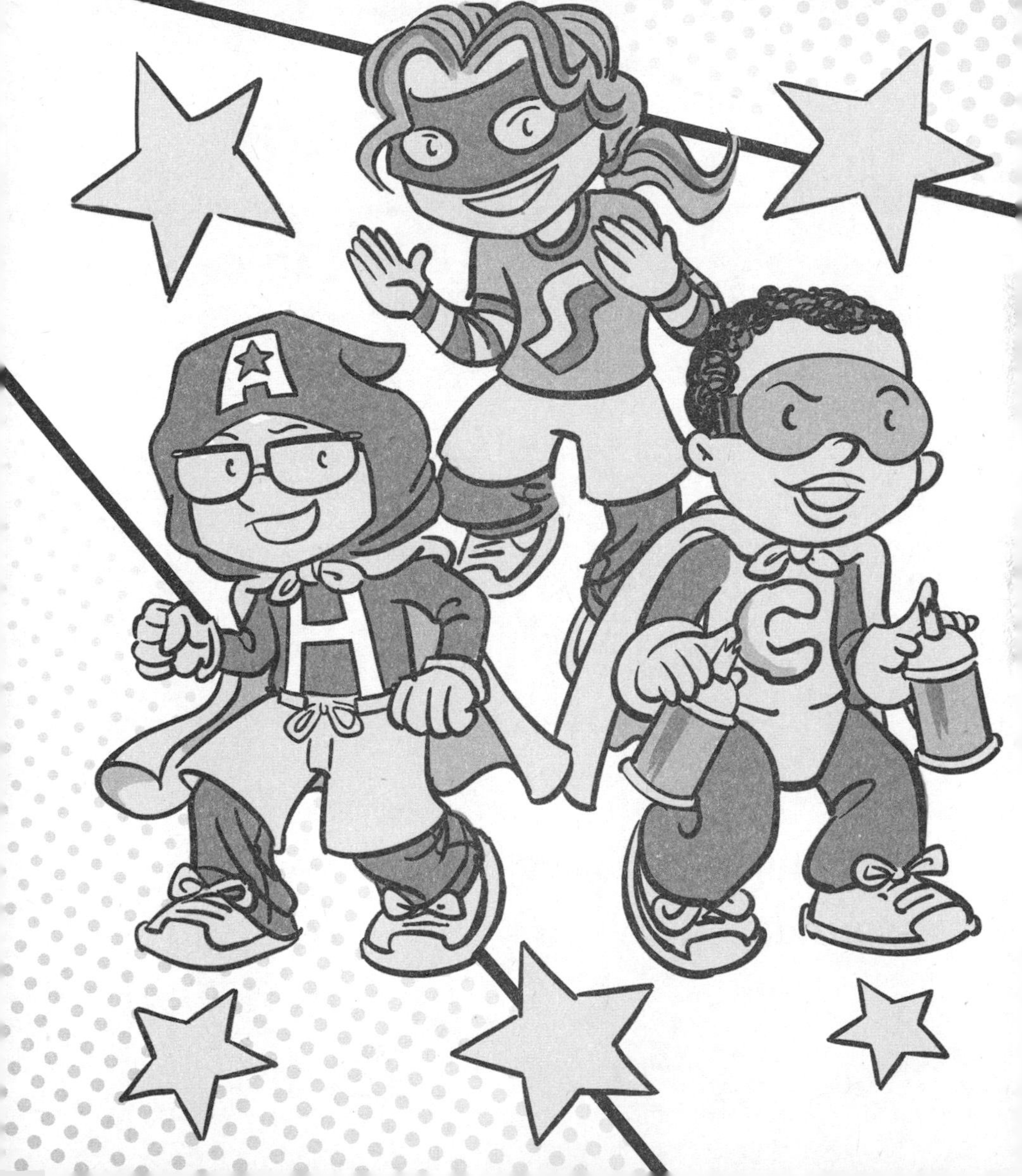
A
A
S
C

CHAPTER 5

The Evil Ice Cream Clone

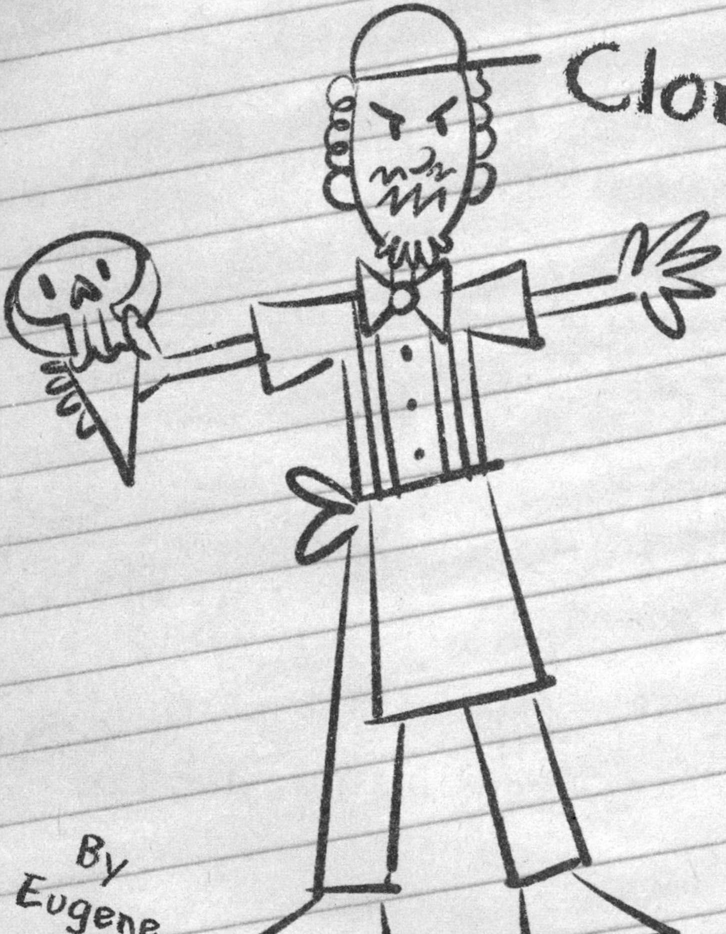

By Eugene

"This meeting of the Sunnyview Superhero Squad has begun! Let's review the super facts . . . ," Eugene announced.

Sally petted Mr. Whiskersworth as she read from her **Supersonic Notebook of Notes**.

"Reasons you think Bob the ice cream truck driver has been replaced by the **Evil Ice Cream Clone**: Bob always had a striped bow tie, but now his bow tie has

polka dots. He isn't wearing his glasses. He didn't stop at the pool. The ice cream truck jingle sounds weird and evil. And he's been driving around the block nonstop."

Sally finished and looked up at Eugene. "That's the cherry on top of the ice cream sundae of clues!" she said. "Bob has definitely turned to the dark side."

TING-TONG! TA-TING! TONG-TONG!

The air filled with an evil sound!

"It's Bob's ice cream truck!" Charlie gasped. "He's come to freeze and hypnotize our brains!"

"Gear up, everyone!" Eugene announced.

BACKPACKS!
CAPES!
SUPERHERO TIME!

Eugene, Charlie, and Sally put on their superhero outfits and became **Captain Awesome, Nacho Cheese Man**, and **Supersonic Sal!**

"Super Goggles, activate!" Captain Awesome then pulled down a pair of goggles from the top of his head.

"Whoa! Cool Super Goggles!" Nacho Cheese Man said. "They look just like your swim goggles."

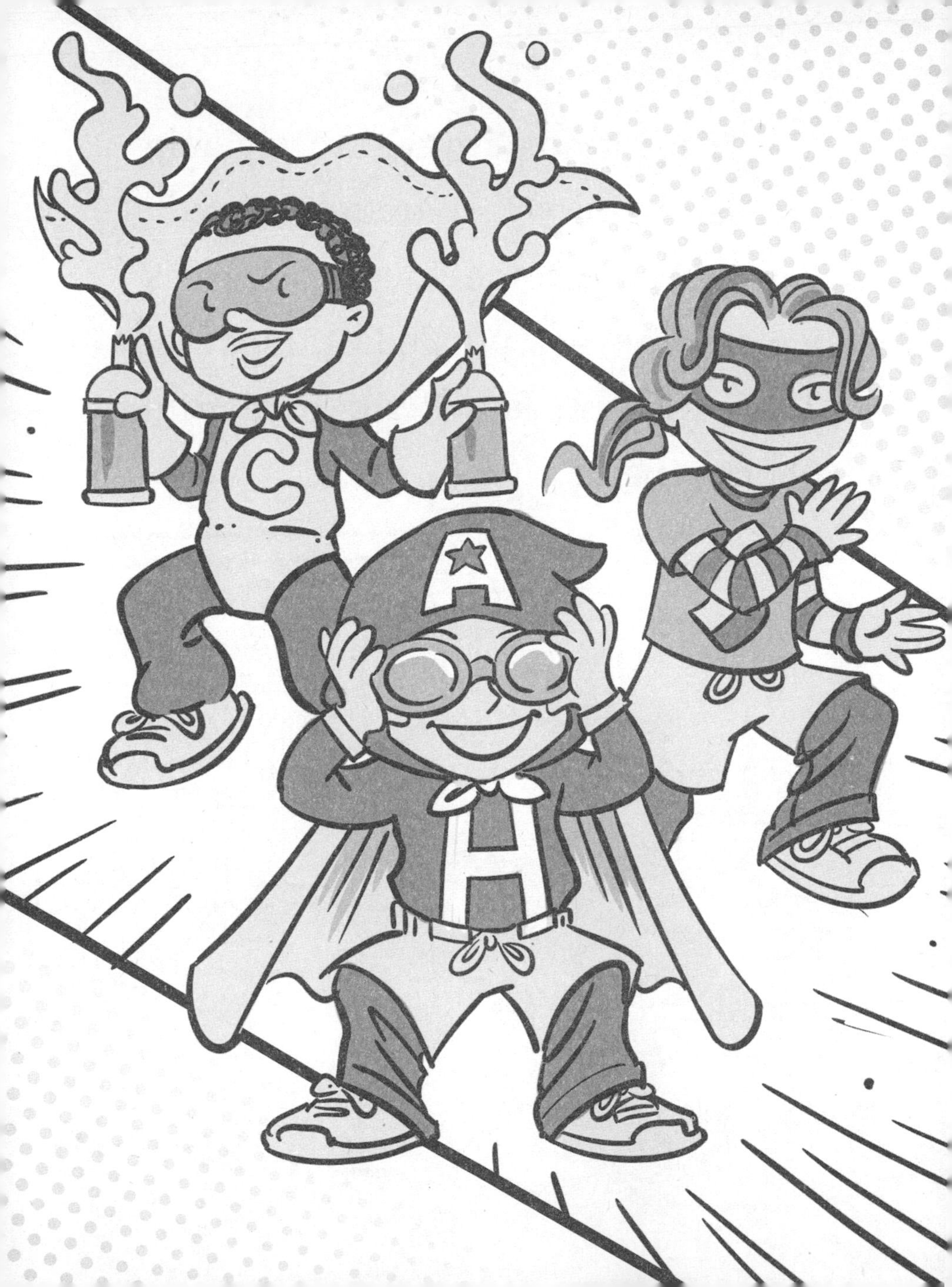

"They kind of are, but they help me see underwater *and* spot evil!" Captain Awesome focused on the ice cream truck parked at the curb. Then the trio snuck up to it and peered inside.

"There's only one way to prove that's the Evil Ice Cream Clone and NOT the real Bob," Supersonic Sal said.

"Put his brain in a glass of lemonade and see if the lemonade gets cold!" Nacho Cheese Man said.

"Okay, never mind. There are *two* ways to prove the ice cream truck driver is the Evil Ice Cream Clone. Since we don't have any lemonade, I'm going to get some ice cream as a test," Supersonic Sal replied.

"If you start feeling icicles in your brain, pat your head and roll on the ground," Captain Awesome said. "That should stop it from taking over your brain."

Supersonic Sal nodded and waited until Bob wasn't looking. Then she grabbed a popsicle that was sitting on the counter and left money for it in the jar.

"That took way too long," Supersonic Sal groaned. "Let me try it before this turns to soup. Tell me if my face starts to freeze."

She licked the ice cream and waited.

"Your face doesn't look frozen," Captain Awesome said, relieved. "How does your brain feel?"

"Pretty brainy," Supersonic Sal said.

"That's good," Captain Awesome replied. "But I don't get it. This can't be it!"

HISSSSSSS!

Mr. Whiskersworth licked some of the melted ice cream on the ground and gave a loud hiss.

"Oh no!" Supersonic Sal cried out. "Mr. Whiskersworth's brain is freezing!"

CHAPTER 6

An Evil Plan Revealed!

By
Eugene

"**Q**uick! Pat his head before his brain freezes!" Captain Awesome gasped.

Supersonic Sal gently patted Mr. Whiskersworth's head.

After a few moments, Mr. Whiskersworth stopped hissing and all was well.

"Whew! That was close," Supersonic Sal said, relieved.

"See? This proves something evil *is* up!" Captain Awesome declared.

"This is just like the time Dr. Snow-It-All used his Jingle Smells to freeze Super Dude's Super Nose in Super Dude number twenty-one!" Nacho Cheese Man reminded them.

"Yes, I remember! Super Dude broke the Jingle Smells with his Super Nose Vibration and defeated Dr. Snow-It-All with a Super Dude Chocolate Melt Shake!" Supersonic Sal added.

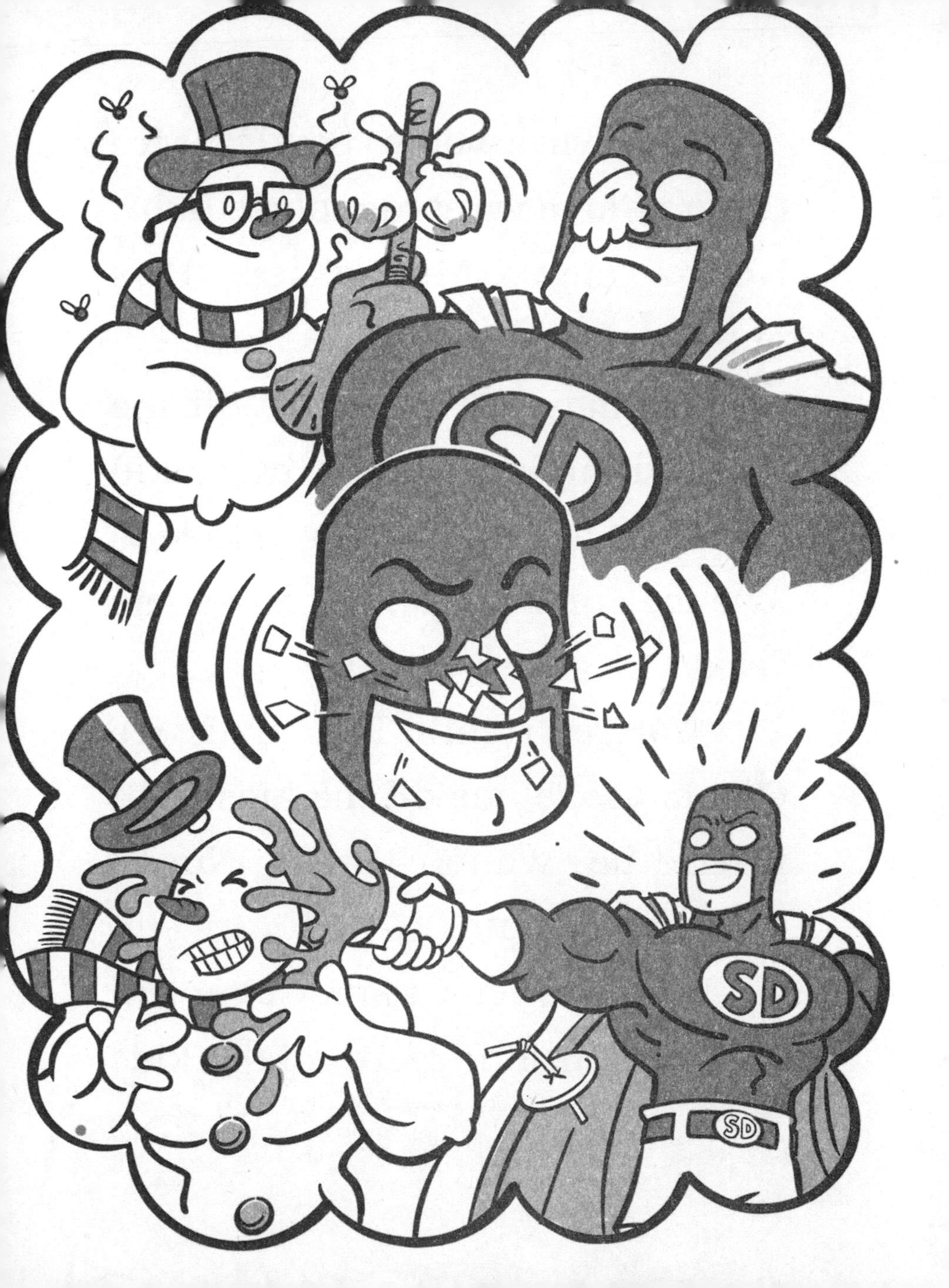
SD
SD
SD

"But why would the Evil Ice Cream Clone want to replace Bob?" Nacho Cheese Man asked. "He's not a superhero."

"He may not be super all the time, but he is a hero to every kid on a hot day like today! All kids love ice cream!" Captain Awesome cried.

"You're right! The Evil Ice Cream Clone has all the kids right where he wants them!" Nacho Cheese Man said.

"The Evil Ice Cream Clone will be able to brain-freeze all the kids

in town . . . maybe even the world . . .
and put them under his brain-freezy
control!" Captain Awesome yelled.

"But why?"

"SO THEY'LL GIVE HIM ALL
THEIR DESSERTS!" the three
heroes realized at the same time.

TING-TONG! TA-TING! TONG-TONG!

The ice cream truck started to pull away from the curb.

"Follow that evil ice cream truck!" Supersonic Sal said, then

hugged Mr. Whiskersworth. "You'd
better go home and take a catnap,
Mr. Whiskersworth. We'll take it
from here."

The cat gave a meow and
trotted back home.

SUPER BIKE TIME!

Captain Awesome hopped on his super-charged Awesome Bike. "Cloaking shields on!" he called out. Then he grabbed some leaves from the bushes and stuck them into his helmet.

Supersonic Sal and Nacho Cheese Man did the same. Then they rode after the truck as fast as they could. If they lost the truck, Sunnyview would be doomed forever.

CHAPTER 7

The Stink of Evil!

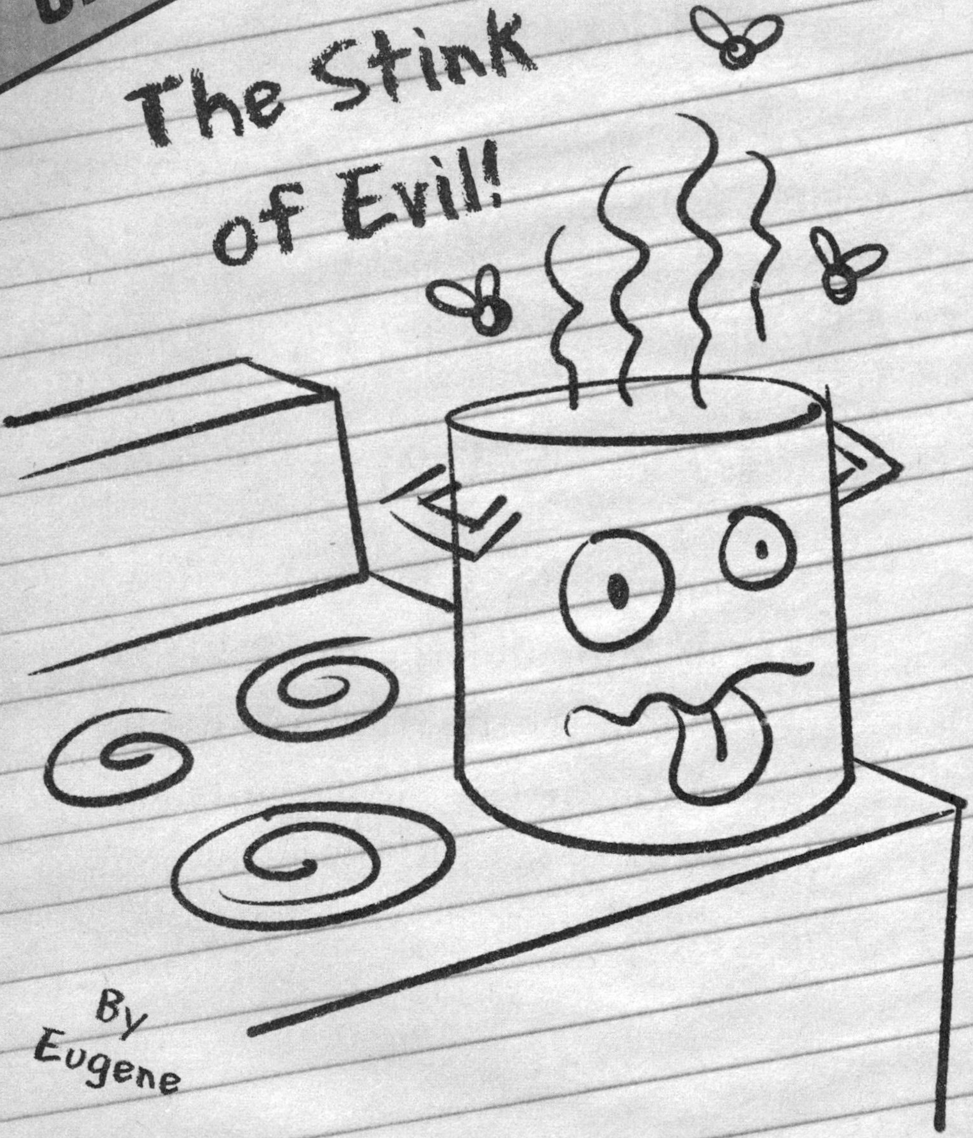

By Eugene

Captain Awesome, Supersonic Sal, and Nacho Cheese Man quietly stopped their Super Bikes at an old storefront. The ice cream truck was parked at the warehouse entrance in the back of the building. The Evil Ice Cream Clone was busy unloading ice cream from the truck.

"There he is!" Supersonic Sal whispered.

"This must be the Ice Cream Clone's evil lair!" Captain Awesome whispered. "There's nothing more evil than evil that doesn't look evil until you realize it's evil!"

The Ice Cream Clone grabbed

a case of Chocoberry Tacos and headed into the old warehouse.

"Now's our chance!" Captain Awesome said. "Come on!"

The three superheroes zipped through the door and almost crashed into a towering stack of boxes.

Supersonic Sal looked up at the flickering dim lights. "It's even more evil-looking on the inside!" Supersonic Sal said.

"At least there are plenty of places to hide," Nacho Cheese Man pointed out.

"It's important to stay unnoticed. But remember what Super Dude always says: 'Superheroes never hide when there's evil to crush!'" Captain Awesome declared.

Nacho Cheese Man gave a dramatic nod. "Less hiding, more evil-crushing. Got it."

Captain Awesome then led them to a brightly lit room in the back of the warehouse, their super senses on high alert. The room had two refrigerators and a stove bigger than any they'd seen before. There were pots, pans, spoons, spatulas, and a spice rack. The three heroes instantly knew where they were.

"Gasp! It's a kitchen of super-bad-guy-ness!" Supersonic Sal whispered.

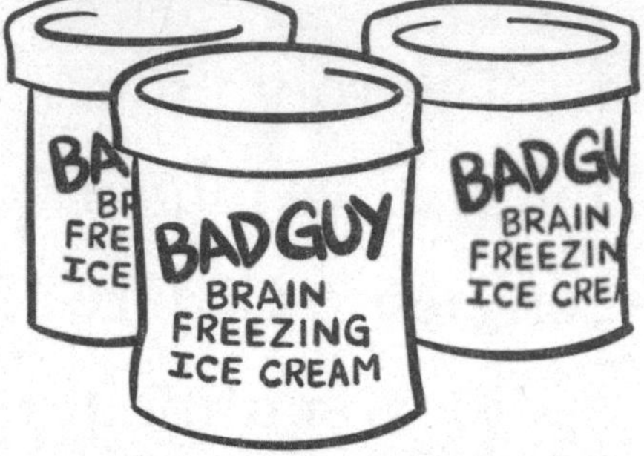
BADGUY
BRAIN
FREEZING
ICE CREAM

"This must be where they make all the bad guy brain-freezing ice cream!" Nacho Cheese Man whispered.

The heroes ducked for cover as the man in the polka-dot bow tie

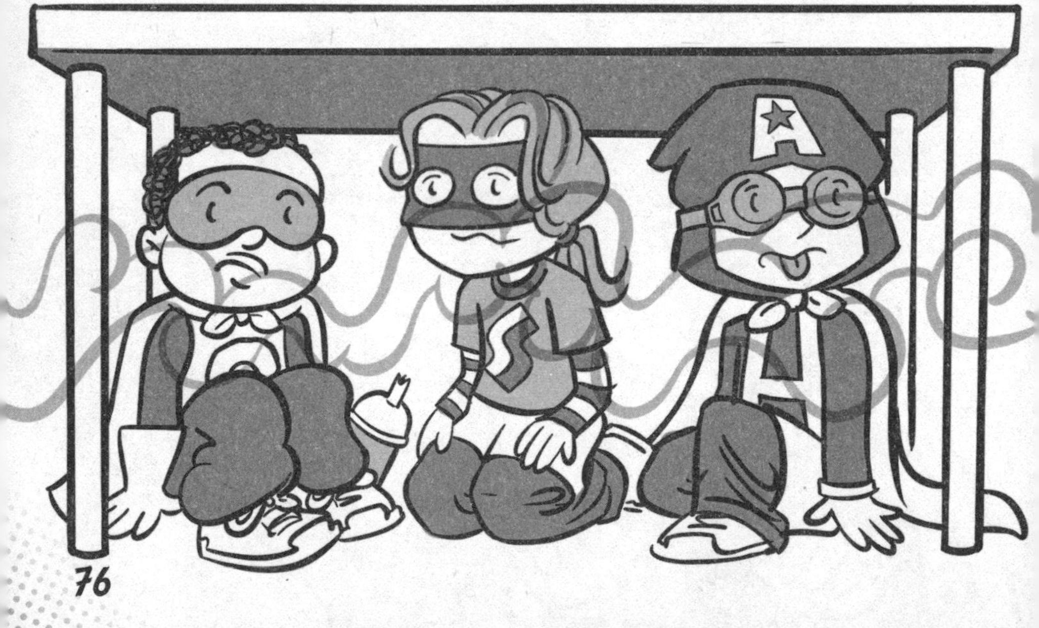

entered the kitchen with a mysterious bowl. He dumped the bowl's contents into a pot on the stove, and the room immediately filled with the stink of rotten onions.

"Ugh! And I thought *broccoli* was bad!" Captain Awesome whispered. "This isn't freezing my brain. . . . IT'S MELTING IT!"

"Quick! Put on my Anti-Stink-Bomb Nose Savers!" Nacho Cheese Man whipped out three clothespins. **PINCH! PINCH! PINCH!**

The trio pinched their noses to avoid the brain-melting stink.

"Good tinking!" Captain Awesome said in a squeaky, nose-pinched voice. "My bain stopped melting!"

"Now butt?" Supersonic Sal asked.

"We need to dop dem from putting dat bain-melting duff into duh ice cream, dat's butt!" Nacho Cheese Man yelled back.

Before the heroes could make their move, another man came into the room wearing the same white outfit with a striped bow tie!

GASP!

SHOCK!

MOUTH DROP!

"It's anudder Evil Ice Cream Clone!" Supersonic Sal said. "And he looks exactly like Bob da ice cream man!"

CHAPTER 8

Send in the Clones

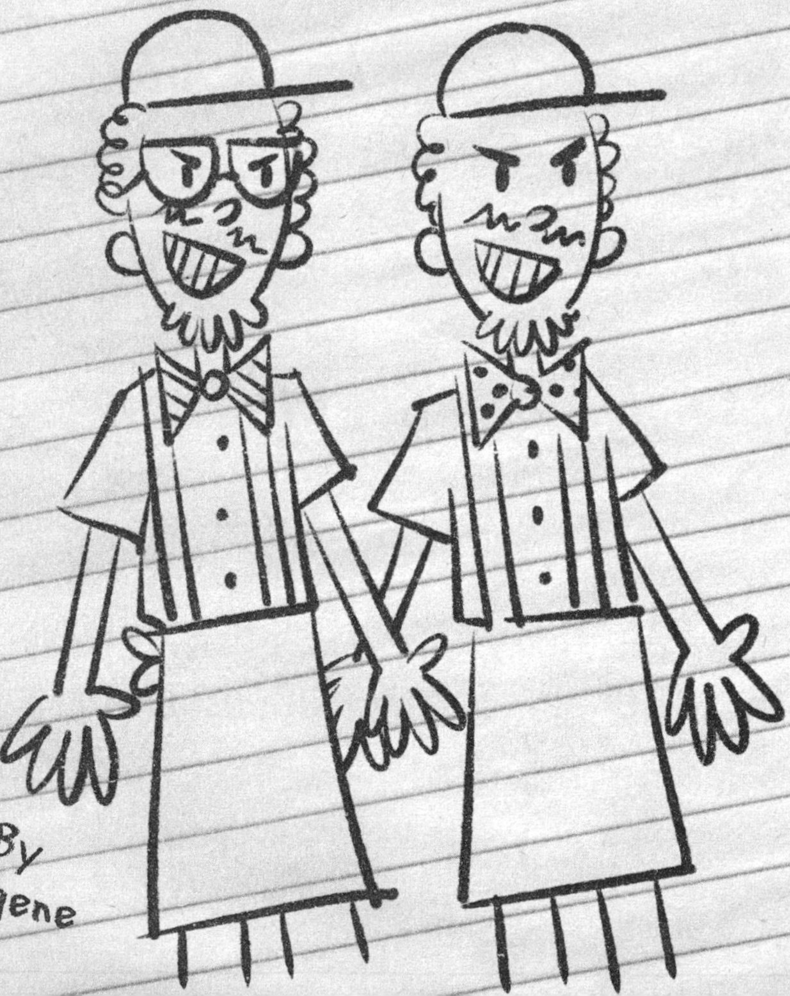

By
Eugene

"**O**n da count of dree we charge dem!" Captain Awesome whispered in the most serious voice he could manage with a clothespin pinching his nose. "UN! DOO! DREE! Gooooo!"

SUPER LEAP!

Captain Awesome, Supersonic Sal, and Nacho Cheese Man jumped from their hiding place, startling the two men.

"Aaaaaah!" the man in the striped bow tie yelped, dropping a box of sprinkles on the floor.

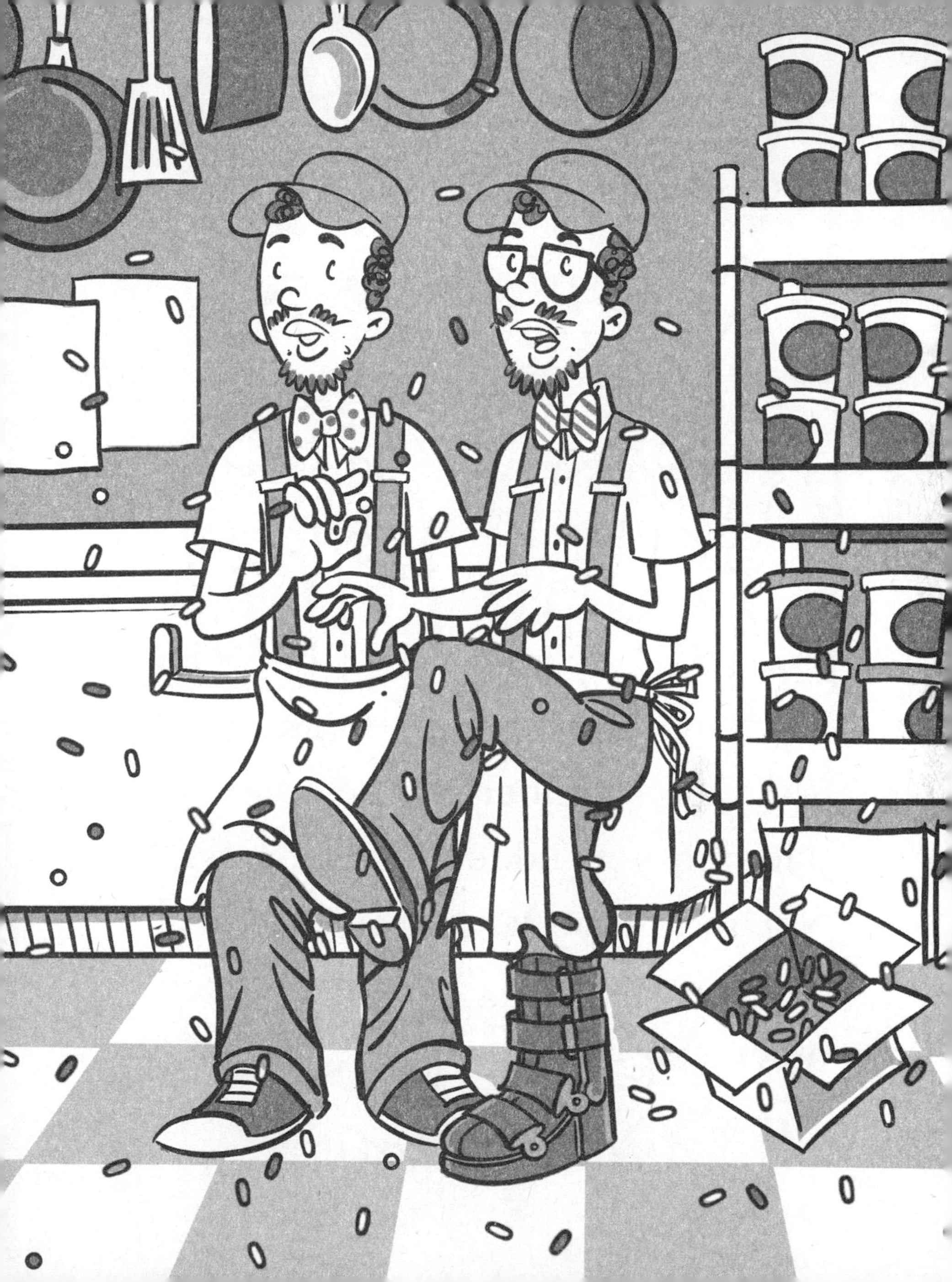

"Dop but you're doing! Duh Suddybew Suberhero Squad is pudding you udder suber arrest!" Nacho Cheese Man shouted.

The two men looked at each other, confused.

"Ummm . . . sorry, but it's hard to understand you with the clothespins on your noses," the man in the polka-dot bow tie said.

"Don't listen to dem. It's a trig to get us to dake off our Anti-Dink-Bomb Dose Sabers," Supersonic Sal warned.

"Don't worry, I'll cheese up first," Nacho Cheese Man replied.

Nacho Cheese Man sprayed some garlic cheese into his mouth and took off his clothespin.

He took a few deep breaths as Captain Awesome and Supersonic Sal watched.

"The sprinkles must've canceled out the brain-melting stink bomb in the bowl," a relieved Nacho Cheese Man said. Then he gave a thumbs-up to his friends.

With that, Captain Awesome and Supersonic Sal took off their Anti-Stink-Bomb Nose Savers as well.

"Cone-gratulations, evil clones! You just got soft-served by the Sunnyview Superhero Squad!" Captain Awesome announced.

"But first! We're going to help you clean up this sprinkle-y mess!"

"What?! We're helping the bad guys?!" Nacho Cheese Man gasped.

"Super Dude said it best in Super Dude number twelve: 'Everyone needs help sometimes. Even the bad guys. And the good

guys are good because they're the ones who help!'" Captain Awesome replied. "CLEANUP POWERS, ACTIVATE!"

"Boy, cleanup powers are the kind of powers I wish I didn't have," Nacho Cheese Man said as he joined his friends.

As he leaned down, Captain Awesome noticed the man with the striped bow tie had a boot on to protect a leg cast. "Did you hurt yourself freezing brains?" Captain Awesome asked.

"Freezing brains? No, I was helping some kids get their kite that was stuck in a tree."

"Okay, and *then* you froze their brains?" Nacho Cheese Man asked.

"No, but I did give them some ice cream, because I'm Bob, the ice cream man. I've seen you heroes around the neighborhood before," Bob answered.

DOUBLE GASP!
DOUBLE SHOCK!
DOUBLE MOUTH DROP!

"I thought YOU were Bob!" Captain Awesome cried, pointing to the man with the polka-dot bow tie.

"Nah. I'm Bob's brother, Rob!" Rob answered. "I was helping my twin brother out while he rested his ankle."

"You're TWINS and NOT the Evil Ice Cream Clone?" Supersonic Sal asked.

"Evil Ice Cream Clone? The only thing maybe evil about Rob is that polka-dot bow tie he likes to wear," Bob said, laughing.

Something still doesn't make sense, Captain Awesome thought. "You may not be titanic twins of evilness, but we've still got a few questions for you!"

CHAPTER 9

A Gelato Fun

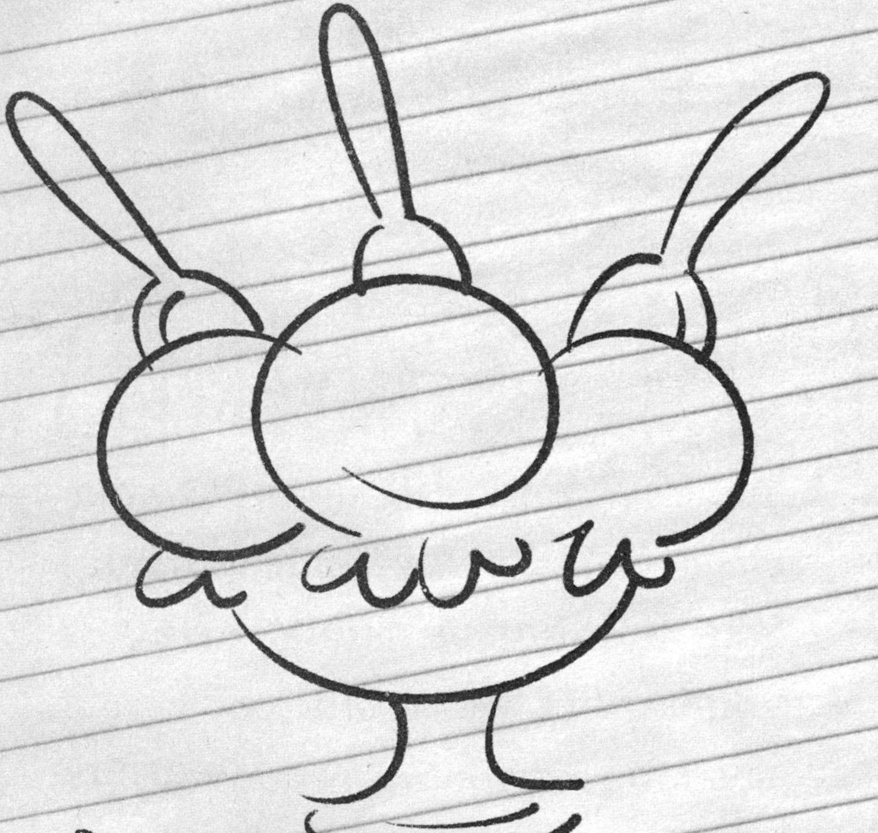

By Eugene

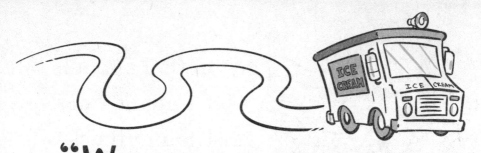

"**W**hy were you driving around and around our neighborhood without stopping?!"

"Why did my cat, Mr. Whiskersworth, get sick?!"

"What's with the evil ice cream truck music?!"

The kids spit out all the questions they had at once.

"Oh, well, I was still learning

my brother's route, and I admit I got lost many times," Rob explained.

"And ice cream isn't very good for animals," Bob added.

"And I think I might have broken the ice cream truck's speaker," Rob added.

"What?! You didn't tell me that!" Bob yelled in surprise.

Captain Awesome picked up the last of the spilled sprinkles and put them in the box. "It looks like we got it wrong. Sorry we thought you were supervillains," he said to Bob and Rob.

"But what was that super-evil smell that was stinking up the place when we got here?" Nacho Cheese Man asked.

"Rob and I are testing out some new ice cream flavors," Bob explained. "We're trying a new ice cream recipe flavored with durian."

"Duri-what?"Captain Awesome asked.

"Durian. It's a tropical fruit that does have a very strong smell. Here. Try a bite."

Rob pulled a carton from the freezer and offered it to the heroes with three spoons. It had a sweet old-oniony smell.

YUCK!
DOUBLE YUCK!
YUUUUUUMMMM!

The strong flavor made Captain
Awesome and Supersonic Sal want
to gag, but Nacho Cheese Man
loved it. "This would go great with
my pepper jack canned cheese!"

Bob then walked over to the counter to grab more new flavors. There was vanilla mint, chocolate raspberry, banana marshmallow, and berry swirl ice cream in every color of the rainbow.

Supersonic Sal paused after tasting the cherry caramel flavor.

"This tastes different from regular ice cream."

"That's because it's gelato, an Italian dessert," Bob said. "It's kind of *like* ice cream, but it has less cream and usually no egg yolks."

Captain Awesome and Nacho Cheese Man dug into it as well.

"Wow! That's really yummy!" Nacho Cheese Man said.

"Well, if you like these flavors, you should come by our new ice cream shop," Rob said. "We're opening it next week."

HOORAYYYYY! ICE CREAM FOR THE WIN!

The three heroes raised their spoons in the air and cheered with delight.

CHAPTER 10

We All Scream for Ice Cream Again!

By
Eugene

After the longest week ever, it was finally SATURDAY NIGHT! Even though tonight wasn't about a birthday cake, a decorated tree, or a carved pumpkin, Eugene was super excited! He and his family finished eating at Super Dude's Pizza Palace, one of his favorite places in town. And now it was time for dessert!

"Next stop, Bob and Rob's Cone Zone!" Eugene's dad announced as they walked over.

It was their opening weekend, and a long line had formed outside the door.

"Wow. This place is already popular!" his mom said.

Eugene scanned the block and spotted Charlie and Sally with their families. It felt like they had to wait for a billion hours, but the three friends finally made it to the front of the line.

Luckily, it was worth the wait. There was more ice cream than they'd ever seen in one place!

"Hey, you three!" Rob said cheerfully. "Welcome to the grand opening of Bob and Rob's Cone Zone! Home of un-CONE-ditional love for all things ice cream!"

The kids laughed and looked up at the menu when they heard a familiar jingle ringing outside.

TING-TING! TA-TING! TING-TING!

"Hey, it's Bob the ice cream man!" Sally said.

"And it sounds like the song is fixed!" Charlie added.

"Yes, hello! Thanks for coming!" Bob said as he climbed down from the truck. "Make sure you try our latest flavors!"

"There's a new flavor?!" Eugene gasped. "Is it Choco-Caramel-Coconut-Cantaloupe Crazy Crunch?!"

"That *does* sound crazy," Bob said. "But I think *our* flavor is even better."

Rob pulled out a red ice cream carton and showed it to the kids.

GASP!
DOUBLE GASP!
JOY!

"STRAWBERRY SUPERHERO SQUAD SURPRISE?!" Eugene, Sally, and Charlie shouted at the same time.

"Yes, it's so strawberry awesome!" Rob said with a smile. "Who'd like to try some?"

"MEEEEE! Me-me-me-me-me-meeee! In a cone, pleeeease!"

LICK! LICK! LICKETY-LICK!

"Wow, I never thought we'd have an ice cream named after us," Sally whispered to her friends.

Eugene and Charlie nodded in excitement.

"It's just like Super Dude said to the healthy Vitamin-C hero when he was being whipped-creamed by the Dessert Devil in Super Dude number four: 'If you keep believing, anything is possible!'"

The kids laughed as Eugene's dad approached the counter.

"I'll have the chocolate gelato," Eugene's dad said. "You know, I've always wondered what the difference between ice cream and gelato is."

Before Rob could answer, Eugene piped in. "Oh! It's made with less cream than ice cream and usually no egg yolks," Eugene said, just like an expert.

Both Rob and Bob perked up as soon as they heard Eugene's answer.

"Yes, that's right!" Rob said.

"We hope you like it," Bob added. "A lot of these flavors are superhero-approved!" Then the brothers gave the trio a secret wink and smile.

So it turns out that the Sunnyview Superhero Squad may not have captured any supervillains or stopped any Evil Ice Cream Clone plans. But they *did* get to eat and inspire some awesome ice cream flavors, and in some ways, that was a lot better *and* yummier.

"Can we come back here every day? Pleeeease?" Eugene asked as he happily licked his ice cream.

By the look on his mom's face, Eugene knew he'd have to eat peas and carrots for the rest of his life if they got ice cream every day. But he was okay with that. Sharing his new favorite ice cream with his best friends was awesome. No, scratch that! It was something *more* awesome than awesome.

It was . . .
MI-TEE!

THE

THE END!